•VOICES IN AFRICAN AN

CIVIL RIGHTS

MODERN CURRICULUM PRESS

◎ Program Consultants

SHARON HARLEY, PH.D.
Associate Professor/Acting Director
African American Studies
University of Maryland

STEPHEN MIDDLETON, PH.D.
Assistant Professor of History
North Carolina University

◎ Program Reviewers

JACOB H. CARRUTHERS, PH.D.
Professor/Associate Director
Center For Inner City Studies
Northeastern Illinois University

BARBARA EMELLE, PH.D.
Associate Director of
Curriculum and Instruction
New Orleans Public Schools

PAUL HILL, JR.
Executive Director,
East End Neighborhood House
Cleveland, Ohio

SUBIRA KIFANO
Teacher Advisor
Language Development Program
  For African American Studies
Los Angeles Public Schools

MARY SHEPHERD LESTER
Director of Mathematics
Dallas Public Schools

LINDA LUPTON
Curriculum Coordinator
Cleveland Public Schools

GWENDOLYN MORRIS
Instructional Support Teacher
Philadelphia Public Schools

THOMASINA PORTIS
Director, Multicultural/Values Education
Washington, D.C. Public Schools

DOROTHY W. RILEY
Librarian and Author
Detroit, Michigan

◎ Illustrators
Louis Pappas, Chapter Bottom Borders; Doug Knutson, 29, 32; Pronto Design and Production, 38-39.

◎ Photo Credits
Bob Adelman/Magnum, 4-5, 44-45; AP/Wide World Photos, Inc., 10, 11, 15, (bottom); 25, 33 (top left), 38 (bottom), 40, 42 (top & bottom left), 43 (top left & bottom right); Eve Arnold/Magnum Photos, Inc., 35 (top right); Gwendolen Cates, 16; Leo Choplin/Black Star, 30-31; Comstock, 43 (bottom middle); Bruce Davidson/Magnum Photos, Inc., 34 (top right); Mary Evans Picture Library/Photo Researchers, Inc., 8 (top); Leonard Freed/Magnum, 38 (top); Lawrence Fried/Magnum Photos, Inc., 43 (middle right); Burt Glinn/Magnum Photos, Inc., 21 (bottom); The Granger Collection, 9 (middle); Jack Moebes/Greensboro Record, 24 (top); Robert L. Haggins, 35 (bottom); Thomas Hoepker/Magnum Photos Inc., 42 (bottom right); Carl Iwasaki/Life Magazine ©1953 Time Inc., 20 (bottom); Bern Keating/Black Star, 9 (top); The Library of Congress/From Photo Researchers, Inc., 6-7; Danny Lyon/Magnum Photos, Inc., 15 (top), 28, 32, 33 (bottom); Charles Moore/Black Star, 34 (bottom left); Courtesy NAACP Public Relations, 8 (bottom), 23 (top), 26; Yoichi R. Okamoto, LBJ Library Collection, 39; Eli Reed/Magnum Photos, Inc., 43 (top right); Ken Regan/Camera 5, 43 (bottom left); Steve Schapiro/Black Star, 36-37; Flip Schulke/Black Star, 17, 35 (top left); UPI/Bettmann, 18-19, 20 (top), 22, 23 (bottom), 24 (bottom), 30 (bottom), UPI/Bettmann Newsphotos/(ACME), 9 (bottom); Fred Ward/Black Star, 13 (bottom), 34 (top left & bottom right); Dan Weiner/Courtesy of Sandra Weiner, 12-13, 14.

◎ Map Credits
Ortelius Design, 27.

◎ Acknowledgments
Every reasonable effort has been made to locate the ownership of copyrighted materials and to make due acknowledgment. Any errors or omissions will gladly be rectified in future editions. p.10: Excerpt from ROSA PARKS: MY STORY by Rosa Parks with Jim Haskins. Published by Penguin USA. pp.22,23,25,32: Excerpts from VOICES OF FREEDOM by Henry Hampton and Steve Fayer with Sarah Flynn. Published by Bantam, Doubleday, Dell Publishing Group, Inc. p. 31: Excerpt from THE EYES ON THE PRIZE CIVIL RIGHTS READER edited by Clayborne Carson, et al. Published by Penguin USA.

Design & Production: TWINC, Catherine Wahl, Kurt Kaptur
Executive Editor: Marty Nordquist
Project Editor: June M. Howland

MODERN CURRICULUM PRESS
299 Jefferson Road, Parisippany, NJ 07054

Simon & Schuster

Based on *The African American Experience: A History* published by Globe Book Company ©1992.

ISBN 0-8136-4975-7 (Reinforced Binding)   ISBN 0-8136-4976-5 (Paperback)

10 9 8 7 6 5 4 3   98 97 96 95

CONTENTS

HISTORY
SPEAKS

Equal rights have been denied to African Americans from the time they first set foot on American shores in the 1600s. Even the Thirteenth Amendment to the *Constitution of the United States* passed in 1865 did not end unfair treatment of them. The Civil War years had seen the first major push for African American freedom and civil rights. The first Civil Rights Act was passed in 1866. For the next hundred years little progress was made. In the mid-1900s, however, African Americans had reached a point where they could no longer wait for equal rights to be given to them. African Americans began to demand their equal rights under the law. A *civil rights movement* was building.

A number of brave people, both African American and white, risked their lives to try to end such things as *segregation* and *discrimination* of African Americans. They held protests and *boycotts*, registered voters, and even worked through the courts to change unfair laws.

All areas of African American life—from where to live to where to go to school to where to work—had been kept "separate but equal." The time for change had come. ✖

1

In the years following World War II, many southern African Americans moved to the North. From 1945-1960 the greatest number of them left the South searching for better jobs, better housing, and a better life. Those who stayed in the South faced harsh segregation laws and customs. Segregation meant that African Americans were kept separate from whites in many public places. A great number of people, not only African Americans, wanted **integration.** *This means all people together, not separated. They also wanted equal rights for all citizens. A civil rights movement grew as people joined together to seek justice.* ⊠

Large signs clearly marked any place or service in the South that was for whites only. Signs marking separate areas for African Americans were also common.

Segregation

Segregation was a fact of life for African Americans in the United States in the mid-1900s. This was not the way they chose to live but rather the way they were forced to live. Black codes, and segregation laws passed after the Civil War such as *Jim Crow laws*, were being enforced in the South.

Jim Crow was a name taken from a popular song, that white people began calling African Americans after the Civil War. This name was used to poke fun at African Americans and to point out that they were different. Jim Crow was later used to refer to anything that kept African Americans and whites separated.

African Americans and whites were kept separate in many public places in the North and South. They went to separate schools. They ate at separate hotels and restaurants. They even drank at separate drinking fountains. African Americans even had to sit at the back on buses. If a bus grew crowded and a white person demanded a seat, an African American who had one had to give it up.

An organization was founded in 1909 to work for fair treatment of African Americans. This *National Association for the Advancement of Colored People (NAACP)* was organized by W.E.B. Du Bois and forty other people, both African American and white. By 1955 the NAACP had over 500,000 members.

Top: The New York office of the NAACP in 1933.
Bottom: The NAACP worked to make improvements in southern classrooms like this one. What can you see that would make studying difficult?

The NAACP has most often fought its battles in court. Many of its cases have gone all the way to the *Supreme Court.* In the beginning this organization worked for fair treatment of African Americans who had been arrested or been victims of illegal violence. Later the organization worked for equality in education, housing, jobs, and voting rights for African Americans. When Rosa Parks joined the group, she didn't know the important part she would play in its work.

When traveling from state to state in the South, African Americans had to sit in their own back section.

Historic Bus Ride

It was a cold evening, December 1, 1955, when Rosa Parks boarded a city bus in Montgomery, Alabama. She did not plan to make history that evening. She was tired from a long day at her sewing machine at the Montgomery Fair department store. Still, Parks could not stop thinking about a weekend meeting to be held by the NAACP. She had been secretary of the NAACP's Montgomery branch since 1943.

She walked down the bus aisle searching for a seat. Parks passed two empty rows in the front of the bus. Those were for white people. According to the law, African Americans could sit starting in the third row, if no whites wanted the seats. Parks took an aisle seat in the third row.

JACKIE ROBINSON

Baseball season—1947—the Brooklyn Dodgers were up to bat. A hush fell over the crowd. The batter swung, hit the ball—it was a home run! For African American Jackie Robinson, it was his first major league home run—but not his last. By playing for the Dodgers, Robinson broke through the wall of segregation that existed in professional sports.

Up until 1947, African Americans had never played on a modern major league baseball team. Robinson was not only the first African American to put on a Dodger uniform. He was also one of the most talented men ever to play the game. This baseball great was named to the Baseball Hall of Fame in 1962.

Soon, the front bus seats were filled and one white man was left standing. The driver stopped the bus and went back where Rosa Parks and other African Americans sat. "Let me have these seats," he said. No one moved at first. "Y'all better make it light on yourselves and let me have those seats."

The other African Americans in the row got up, but Parks did not. She was tired, but that was not the only reason why she did not move. "The only tired I was," she said later, "was tired of giving in. I wanted to be treated like a human being."

The angry driver left the bus and came back with two police officers. One asked Parks why she would not stand. She asked him, "Why do you all push us around?"

"I don't know," the policeman answered, "but the law is the law, and you are under arrest."

After her arrest Rosa Parks was taken to the police station. What is happening to her here?

Rosa Parks was escorted to her legal hearings by NAACP officials.

Organizing a Boycott

Rosa Parks' brave act set in motion a series of events that would change American history forever. The NAACP had been looking for a *test case* to challenge Montgomery's bus segregation law. This law kept African Americans separate from whites on buses. The NAACP believed these segregation laws were against the rights stated in the *Constitution of the United States.*

The case of Rosa Parks would be used to challenge the bus law in court. Rosa Parks knew that by going to trial, she would be found guilty. However, then NAACP lawyers would argue that the law was unfair and should be changed. They were prepared to take her case all the way to the Supreme Court. A ruling from this court would affect the rights of African Americans all over the country.

EQUAL RIGHTS FOR ALL

The *Constitution of the United States* begins, "We, the people. . . ." Some additions, or amendments, have been made to it to make sure that "we the people" includes people of all races. Which of these amendments did the Montgomery bus law violate?

Amendment 13
Neither slavery nor involuntary servitude . . . shall exist within the United States. . . .

Amendment 14
All persons born or naturalized in the United States . . . are citizens of the United States and of the State wherein they reside. No State shall make or enforce any law which shall abridge [cut off] the privileges or immunities of citizens of the United States; nor shall any State deprive any person of life, liberty, or property, without due process of law; nor deny to any person within its jurisdiction the equal protection of the laws.

Amendment 15
The right of citizens of the United States to vote shall not be denied or abridged by the United States or by any State on account of race, color, or previous condition of servitude.

Martin Luther King, Jr. spoke to
boycotters in Montgomery,
Alabama.

A group of African American ministers organized a
one-day bus boycott to show anger over Rosa Parks'
arrest. They planned that all the African Americans who
usually rode the buses would not on that day. Almost
three-quarters of bus riders in Montgomery were
African American. A boycott would cost the bus company a great deal of money.

The ministers, who later formed the *Montgomery
Improvement Association (MIA)*, planned the boycott
for December 5, 1955, the day of Rosa Parks' trial. The
organizers were unsure if all African Americans in the
city would join the protest. However, on the morning of
December 5, the entire African American community
filled Montgomery's sidewalks. Some of them were
walking. Some stood waiting for "taxis," or rides from

friends with cars. However, none of them boarded buses. It was the first public showing of African American unity in the community.

The trial of Rosa Parks was completed quickly and the expected verdict was announced—guilty. Martin Luther King, Jr. called for a mass meeting about the boycott for that evening. Thousands of African Americans attended. The MIA put loudspeakers on the lawn of the church where they were meting so all could hear King speak. "The great glory of American democracy is the right to protest," he said. He also spoke about the importance of protesting with love, not violence. His speech encouraged everyone to continue the boycott, and they did.

Boycotters of Montgomery waited for car pool "taxis" to carry them to work.

A Long Walk to Victory

Montgomery's African Americans faced a difficult test in the months that followed. Buses were the major form of transportation. African Americans who owned taxis offered rides when they could. The few African Americans who owned cars formed volunteer car pools. They set up a system that carried about 30,000 people to and from work each day. This system was supported by some whites of Montgomery, also.

Some of the boycotters had more to worry about than finding a ride to work or to school. Rosa Parks lost her job. Bricks were thrown through the windows of many African American homes. A number of the boycotters were threatened with violence and Martin Luther King, Jr.'s home was firebombed. However, none of these actions stopped the boycott.

Much of the violence came from white people in a group called the *Ku Klux Klan.* The Klan, formed right after the Civil War, was a secret society. Its members believed that only white people who had certain beliefs or backgrounds should have equal rights or power in America. Wearing white hoods and robes, they often caused terror and violence in the African American community. With no regard for the law, the Klan often claimed responsibility for cross burnings, beatings, house burnings, and even murders.

Meanwhile, the case of Rosa Parks moved slowly through the courts. Finally, on November 13, 1956, the *justices* of the Supreme Court decided that the Montgomery bus segregation law violated the Constitution. They ruled that segregation on buses was not legal. Integration must take its place.

Top:
How do you know these men belong to the Ku Klux Klan?
Bottom:
Klan members burn a cross at a late-night meeting in Jacksonville, Florida.

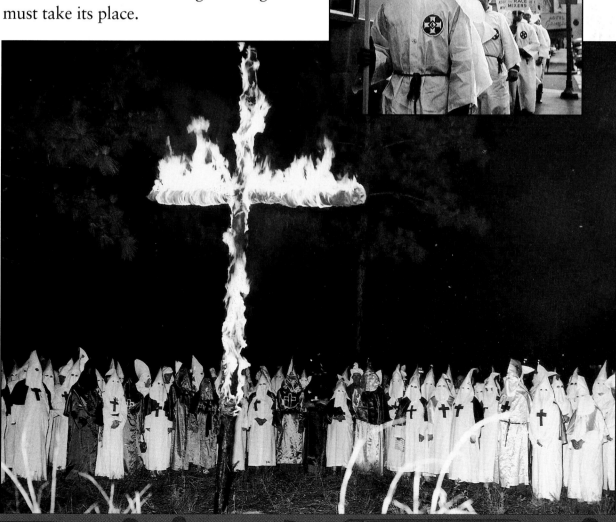

The Montgomery boycott had gone on for over a year. In the end it cost the bus company over two-thirds of its profit.

Rosa Parks continues to teach young people about civil rights history. These students were part of the Reverse Freedom Tour. Find out more about it.

The leaders of the Montgomery boycott continued their efforts in other cities in the South. Protests against segregation took many forms as the civil rights movement continued.

After the Supreme Court ruling, Rosa Parks and her husband still feared for their safety. They moved to Detroit, Michigan, in 1957. In the years that followed, Parks traveled all over the country talking about her experiences. She later founded the Rosa and Raymond Parks Institute for Self-Development. In 1992 she published a book telling about those days in Montgomery. The city honored her also. The bus on which Rosa was arrested traveled along Cleveland Avenue. That street was renamed Rosa Parks Boulevard. ✶

TALK ABOUT IT

◎ Rosa Parks is a heroine to many people. What character traits does she have that make her a heroine? Whom do you admire or look up to as a hero or heroine? What makes that person so special?

◎ Why do you think so many African Americans in Montgomery took part in the boycott? How have people in your city or community worked to change a law? How successful were they?

◎ How do you think Rosa Parks felt after she was arrested? If you could talk with her, what is one question you would ask her about that time in her life?

WRITE ABOUT IT

Read more about the Montgomery boycott, and try to feel what it was like to be part of this history-making event. Put yourself in the place of an African American citizen of Montgomery, in 1955. Write a letter to a friend or relative in another part of the United States. Explain all about the bus boycott, and how it was organized. Are you going to join in? Why or why not?

2

With Martin Luther King, Jr. as its leader, the **Southern Christian Leadership Conference (SCLC)** set up plans for more nonviolent actions for change like the boycotts. Attempts to push for equal rights would take different forms also. One struggle started that same year in Little Rock, Arkansas, not on buses, but in schools. Many who worked there for equality in Little Rock were still in their teens. ✠

Some citizens of Little Rock, Arkansas protested loudly when the government ordered them to allow African American students to attend all-white schools.

THE "LITTLE ROCK NINE"

Starting at a new school is never easy. However, few students have had to live through what happened to fifteen-year-old Elizabeth Eckford on September 4, 1957.

That day a sea of angry white faces met Eckford when she got off the bus a block from her school. Not only was it the first day of school in Little Rock, Arkansas. It was also the first time an African American student would attend the all-white Central High School. The jeering and screaming mob tried to block Elizabeth's path. All alone, with knees shaking, she started walking toward the school. "It was the longest block I ever walked in my whole life," she said later.

ONE GIRL MAKES A DIFFERENCE

Because of seven-year-old Linda Brown, other African American children were legally allowed to attend any and all public schools in the United States starting in 1954.

The legal case started when Linda and her father, Reverend Oliver Brown, of Topeka, Kansas sued the Board of Education there. Reverend Brown wanted Linda to go to an all-white school in their neighborhood rather than be bussed across town to another school. Topeka schools were segregated.

The case was brought before the Supreme Court where the justices handed down the famous *Brown v. Board of Education* decision. In it they stated that school segregation because of race was unconstitutional. It was the first legal ruling that said African Americans must be given the opportunity to attend the same schools as white students.

Elizabeth Eckford is directed by National Guardsmen in Little Rock.

Elizabeth was not supposed to be alone that morning. Eight other students, all later called the "Little Rock Nine" had agreed to start school at Central High that day. At the last minute, it was decided that the students should arrive together and go into the school by the rear door. Elizabeth was not told of this change in plans because her family did not have a telephone.

The enrollment of African American students in all-white schools was one thing for which the NAACP had fought long and hard. On May 17, 1954, in the case of *Brown v. Board of Education* (Brown against the Board of Education), the U.S. Supreme Court had ruled that segregation in schools was illegal.

In the court's decision, Chief Justice Earl Warren wrote that "separate" could never be "equal" in education or any other part of public life. For African Americans to receive an equal education, they must not be kept separate. The schools must be integrated.

The First Try

Many southern states did not agree with the Supreme Court ruling and took a stand against the integration of schools. That September, in 1957, Arkansas governor Orval Faubus announced that he was sending state National Guard troops to Central High to protect the African American students.

When Elizabeth Eckford approached the front door of Central High that day, however, the soldiers raised their guns and blocked her path. They would not let her enter. The governor later defended their actions by stating they were protecting Eckford by keeping her out of the school.

Elizabeth could do nothing but walk back through the angry mob and away from the school. Through all the shoving and threatening, she was able to reach the bus stop. A white male reporter and a white woman helped Elizabeth board the bus and reach home safely.

African American students enter Little Rock's Central High. How does this scene compare to the normal scene outside of your school?

THE SUPREME JUDGE

The first African American named to the U.S. Supreme Court was Thurgood Marshall. Appointed in 1967 by President Lyndon Johnson, Marshall served on the bench for thirty-four years.

Thurgood Marshall was born in Baltimore, Maryland, in 1908 and died in 1993. He received his law degree from Howard University Law School.

In 1932, Marshall became the chief lawyer for the NAACP. His main goal was to have a previous Supreme Court ruling, *Plessy v. Ferguson,* overturned. This ruling said that "separate but equal" facilities in the United States were legal. Marshall and the NAACP knew this law had to be changed if African Americans were ever to receive equal civil rights. Marshall reached his goal. In 1954, he successfully argued the *Brown v. Board of Education* case which called for an end to segregation in public schools. It overturned the *Plessy v. Ferguson* ruling.

What other important legal cases was Thurgood Marshall (back row, far right) a part of? Why not find out?

The Arkansas governor kept Central High closed for almost a month. Then, on September 24, the nine African American students tried again to enter the school. As before a mob had gathered but the students successfully reached the school's side door. President Dwight Eisenhower had taken the control of the soldiers away from the governor. He commanded them to protect the students both inside and outside of the school.

The nine students were escorted to school every day for months afterward, always entering by the front door. Students had to become used to attending classes with soldiers in the hallways and at the doors of their school. As Melba Patillo, an African student put it, "I went in not through the side doors, but up the front stairs, and there was a feeling of pride and hope that yes, this is the United States; yes, there is a reason I salute the flag; and it's going to be okay."

However, the African American students still faced problems. The new students were often cursed at, pushed, and kicked by white students. "Every morning for nine months we got up, polished our saddle shoes—and went to war," Melba said. With amazing courage

Top: "The Little Rock Nine" with NAACP leaders who helped them attend Central High.
Bottom: African students often faced yelling crowds while waiting for the school bus.

and supported by their families and African American community, they remained in school.

On May 27, 1958, Ernest Green, one of the Little Rock Nine, became the first African American to graduate from Central High. Green said later, "I knew that once I . . . received that diploma, . . . I had cracked the wall. . . . I had accomplished what I had come there for."

Top: North Carolina students (left to right): D. Richmond, Franklin McCain, E. Blair, Jr., and J. McNeil.
Bottom: Sit-in demonstration at Woolworth's.

Student Sit-ins

Other areas of daily life in the South were slow to change from segregation to integration. The SCLC, made up of civil rights leaders from all over the South, was formed in 1957. Students were also making civil rights history, becoming one of the leading forces of the movement. In 1960, four African American college students held a new kind of protest in an F. W. Woolworth's store in Greensboro, North Carolina.

The students met one winter night at North Carolina Agricultural and Technical College. Joseph McNeil, Ezell Blair, Jr., Franklin McCain, and David Richmond talked about the brave people who were protesting segregation. "I was particularly inspired by the people in Little

Rock," Joe McNeil said later. "I was really impressed with the courage that those kids had."

The four planned something to show their own support for the civil rights movement. Together, the college students would go to eat at the F.W. Woolworth's lunch counter. However, they knew the lunch counter was segregated and they would not be served any food. F. W. Woolworth's allowed African Americans to shop in the store, but would not let them eat there. The four men agreed to protest this policy.

This plan, called a *sit-in*, was not meant to cause a disturbance or make trouble. McNeil and the others thought that just by sitting at the counter, they could make people see how senseless segregation was.

The day of their sit-in, everything went just as the four students had expected. They bought some items and then sat down at Woolworth's lunch counter. McNeil and the others were not served although they stayed seated until the store closed.

Local newspapers carried the story the next day. Support for their protest grew. When they returned to the store in following days, as many as one thousand people crowded in and around the store.

A sit-in at Jackson, Mississippi. If you were one of the protesters, how would you feel?

HOW TO BEHAVE AT A SIT-IN

All students participating in the Nashville sit-ins were given the following directions, written by the National Student Movement:

DO show yourself in a friendly way at all times.

DO sit straight and always face the counter.

DO refer all information to your leader in a polite manner.

DO remember the teachings of Jesus Christ, Mohandas Gandhi, and Martin Luther King, Jr.

DON'T strike back or curse back if attacked.

DON'T laugh out loud.

DON'T hold conversations with floorwalkers.

DON'T leave your seat until your leader has given you permission.

DON'T block entrances or aisles of the store.

Why do you think leaders suggested these rules to students?

The tale of this quiet protest spread to newspapers all over the country. The scene was repeated by groups of students in Nashville, Tennessee, and other southern cities where sit-ins were held. Sometimes protesters had food dumped on them or were threatened. Always they remained seated and quiet.

Students participating in the sit-ins showed the strength of the young African American community. They were not content to let the adults solve problems that also affected them. Students were guided in their protests, however. Nonviolence was the important idea.

Diane Nash, a college student and leader of the Nashville demonstrations, summed up the purpose of the nonviolent direct-action protests. Her ideas are similar to those suggested by Dr. King and other leaders.

Protesters picketed outside of Woolworth stores in the North.

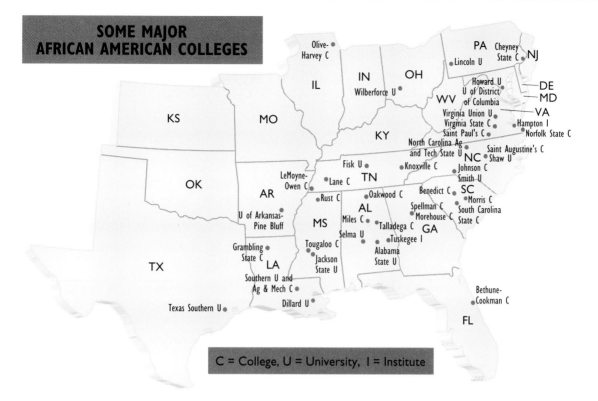

SOME MAJOR AFRICAN AMERICAN COLLEGES

Olive-Harvey C

PA Cheyney State C NJ

Lincoln U

IL IN OH

Wilberforce U

Howard U
U of District of Columbia

WV

DE
MD
VA

Virginia Union U
Virginia State C
Saint Paul's C

Hampton I
Norfolk State C

KS MO

KY

North Carolina Ag and Tech State U

Saint Augustine's C

Fisk U Knoxville C NC Shaw U

Johnson C
Smith U

LeMoyne-Owen C Lane C TN

Benedict C SC

OK AR

Rust C

Oakwood C

Morris C
South Carolina State C

Spellman C
Morehouse C

U of Arkansas-Pine Bluff

AL

Miles C

MS

Talladega C GA

Selma U

Tuskegee I

Tougaloo C

Alabama State U

Grambling State C LA

Jackson State U

TX

Southern U and Ag & Mech C

Bethune-Cookman C

Texas Southern U

Dillard U

FL

C = College, U = University, I = Institute

Nash encouraged students to follow this procedure when confronting segregation problems:

- Investigate — Find out exactly what the problem is and why it is happening.
- Educate — Give everyone in your group as much information as you can find about the problem.
- Negotiate — Meet with people who oppose you. Let them know your feelings and demands. Try to work out an agreement through discussion.
- Demonstrate — Let the rest of the community know about the problem and how you believe it should be solved.
- Resist — If the system does not change, refuse to support it.

Students all over the South soon began to stage sit-ins, read-ins, and other protests. In the North, students also took action to support the movement. They *picketed* F. W. Woolworth's and other stores in support of the southern students.

The students' fight for integration slowly succeeded. Because of their efforts, the lunch counters in Greensboro and Nashville began serving African Americans. Restaurants, hotels, and other public places in many cities of the South slowly became integrated. These were important steps forward for the civil rights movement.

In April of 1960, several hundred African American students from twelve southern states gathered at Shaw University in Raleigh, North Carolina. There they formed an important youth organization, the *Student Nonviolent Coordinating Committee*.

The SNCC took a new approach in organizing African Americans. Since it was meant to be an organization of young people, SNCC representatives went to talk students. They visited high schools, colleges, and churches to help young people form groups of their own.

Since music brought people together, it was often a part of SNCC meetings. To help them inspire people and raise money, the SNCC Freedom Singers were organized in 1962. This chorus of young men and women used music to reach out to the people and bring them together. The Freedom Singers performed at civil rights gatherings all over the country.

What do you think these Freedom Singers are singing about?

TALK ABOUT IT

◎ Why do you think the citizens of Little Rock reacted so violently to African American students attending Central High? Since most protesters were not students themselves, why were they so concerned?

◎ Describe how you think the nine African American students felt after their first week at Central High. How would you have felt? How does their treatment compare with how new students are treated in your school?

◎ Why do you think sit-ins were successful in bringing about changes in segregation? Where might a sit-in be used today to change something in your community?

WRITE ABOUT IT

Think of a law or a custom in your community that you might want to change. Choose a law that has to do with allowing or not allowing people to do something that you feel strongly about. What could you and other students do to bring about the change you want? Write a plan of action for achieving this change that you might put on a poster or flyer. Make your message exciting enough that other students will want to join your plan.

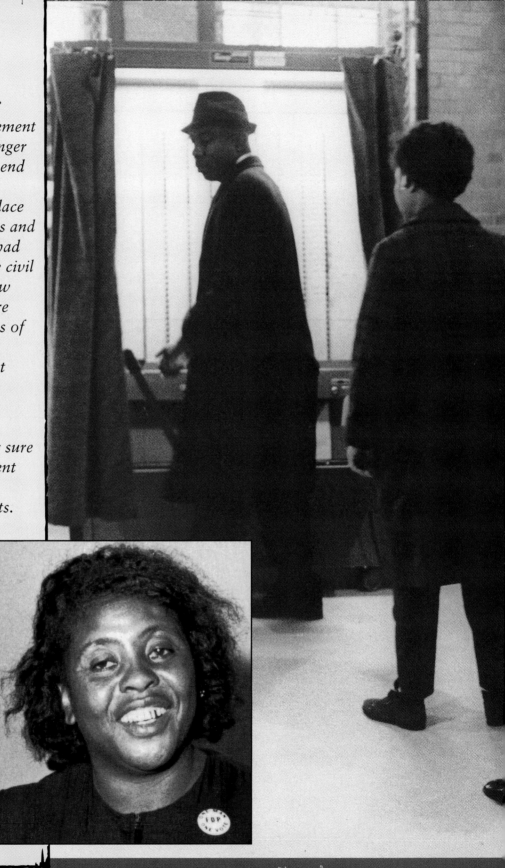

3

The civil rights movement grew larger and stronger in the 1960s. By the end of 1963, some 930 protests had taken place in 115 southern cities and over 20,000 people had been arrested. As the civil rights movement grew violence became more common. The actions of protesters became focused on important goals. One was registering African Americans to vote. Another was making sure the federal government passed new laws to protect citizens' rights. African Americans would no longer be denied the rights they deserved under the law ✠

Southern voters and Fannie Lou Hamer (Inset) were among the large numbers of African Americans who used their right to vote as soon as they were able.

A Brave Decision

Fannie Lou Hamer was one African American who learned surprising information at a SNCC meeting in 1962. "Until then . . . I didn't know that a *Negro* could register and vote," she said later. Hamer grew up in Sunflower County, Mississippi where her family were *sharecroppers*. Hamer's life was filled with hard work, poor pay and no hope of things getting better.

When Hamer realized she had the right to vote, she decided to register. This was a dangerous decision. In most southern cities, African Americans were discouraged from voting by being turned away from registration or threatened or made to pass very difficult tests. This did not stop Fannie Lou Hamer.

"What was the point of being scared?" she asked. "The only thing they could do to me was kill me and it seemed like they'd been trying to do that a little bit at a time ever since I could remember."

Volunteers visited Africans in their homes to register them to vote.

On August 31, 1962, Hamer and about twenty other African Americans stood in line in the hot sun waiting to register to vote. Once inside, they struggled with a difficult, 22-question test. After finally registering and returning home, Hamer was met by the owner of the land her family farmed. He threatened to fire Hamer and force her family off his land unless she removed her name from the registration list. "No," she told him. "I didn't register for you. I registered for myself." She and her family left Sunflower County.

From that point on, Fannie Lou Hamer became a constant worker for civil rights. In 1964, when the Democratic Party in Mississippi turned away African Americans, she formed the Mississippi Freedom Democratic

Fannie Lou Hamer at the 1964 Democratic Convention.

party. "The question for Black people is not when is the white man going to give us our rights," she said. "We have to take {our rights} for ourselves."

In the early 1960s the SCLC, SNCC, and other civil rights groups sent workers, many of them white, all through the South. Their goal was to register African Americans to vote. Many of these workers were arrested or beaten. Some were even killed. All found resistance and trouble everywhere they went. Still, they kept on with their registration efforts.

Voters practice casting their ballots in the Freedom Vote held by registration workers.

Protesters from all parts of the United States took part in the March on Washington. What do the signs they carried tell you about them?

The March on Washington

In the summer of 1963 the word had gone out across the country. An important protest march had been planned. From Harlem to the crowded streets of Los Angeles, supporters of the civil rights movement took notice. They were all headed for Washington, D.C., the site of the planned march. Civil rights supporters of every race and religion packed their bags and traveled to the nation's capital.

Some would travel by train and plane—some by chartered bus—some by car caravan. People of all ages started on a journey that would change the face of America forever.

The March on Washington, as it was called, had been planned for a specific reason. President John F. Kennedy had presented a new civil rights bill to Congress. The bill called for an end to discrimination in schools, housing, and work places. The bill had not yet been passed by Congress and many doubted that it would be. Civil rights leaders hoped that a mass march showing support for the bill would put pressure on Congress to pass it. The NAACP, SCLC, SNCC, and most other civil rights groups agreed to take part.

There was one important civil rights leader who did not take part in the March on Washington. He said it was a "sellout" and a "takeover" by white people. He was Malcolm X.

Malcolm X addresses a freedom rally in Harlem.

CULTURE CORNER

ON THE BIG SCREEN

The theater lights go down. Across the screen flashes the forceful image of Malcolm X. He was a big man with big ideas.

Al Hajj Malik Shabazz, better known as Malcolm X, had a growing audience for his ideas. Film producer and director Spike Lee made a feature film about Malcolm X. Lee wanted the younger generation of African Americans to know more about this man who had spoken out about the power of self-esteem. This film is part of a growing number of motion pictures about African Americans.

Many young people have already read Malcolm X's important book, *The Autobiography of Malcolm X*. More and more African Americans are discovering and following this philosopher's belief in African American unity and pride. Some have even chosen to put his name on their clothing, posters, and jewelry.

Born Malcolm Little, in Omaha, Nebraska, in 1925, Malcolm X took that name when he joined the **Black Muslims** in 1952. Most civil rights leaders believed that having an integrated society was the most important step toward gaining civil rights. At the time of the march, Malcolm X was very concerned about the unfair treatment of African Americans. However, he believed that the only way to gain equal rights was to develop economic independence within the African American community. He encouraged young African Americans to think of themselves as part of a majority, not a minority.

He eventually made a holy trip, or hajj, to *Mecca* in 1964, and began to change his views. He focused more on building African American pride. Before he could do much about his changed ideas, he was *assassinated,* in 1965.

What do you suppose lawmakers thought when they saw this crowd gathered at the March on Washington?

Three other leaders shaped the famous march. One was A. Philip Randolph. Randolph had planned a March on Washington in 1941 that was never held. President Franklin Roosevelt was so worried about the power of such a march, he gave in to Randolph's demands. Another leader was John Lewis, a fiery member of the SNCC. The third was Martin Luther King, Jr.

The morning of August 28 was hot and sunny. More than 250,000 people had poured into the capital. This would be the largest demonstration for equal rights the country had ever seen. The people who gathered formed a sea of faces around the Washington Monument's reflecting pool. Together they walked to the Lincoln Memorial carrying signs and singing. There they rested and listened to King and the other speakers.

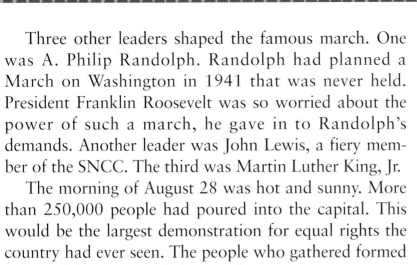

The people in the March on Washington carried protest signs. These signs told their feelings on many issues. How do you think these issues compare with things that people are worried about today?

Marchers sang "We Shall Overcome" and other songs.

Millions of people around the world heard King's "I Have a Dream" speech on radio and television. He said his dream was the same dream that many Americans had. Didn't all Americans want to be treated fairly and equally?

The response from the crowd was tremendous. Ralph Abernathy, who had worked with King since the Montgomery days, was at the march. He spoke for many when he said, "This was the greatest day of my life."

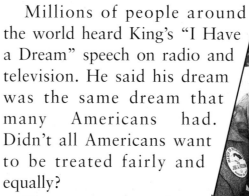

WE DEMAND
DECENT HOUSING NOW!

WE DEMAND
VOTING RIGHTS NOW!

END SEGREGATED RULES IN PUBLIC SCHOOLS!

WE MARCH FOR JOBS FOR ALL NOW!

Martin Luther King, Jr. giving his "I Have a Dream" speech.

Civil rights leaders watch President Johnson sign the Voting Rights Act of 1965.

The March on Washington was important for several reasons. It gave African Americans hope for a brighter future. Also, it clearly defined the civil rights movement for other Americans. Following the march, many people volunteered to fight for passage of the *Civil Rights Act*. Finally, the march convinced members of Congress that a law dealing with civil rights was needed and wanted by the people.

However, the Civil Rights Act did not became law until July 1964, eight months after President Kennedy's assassination shocked the nation. President Lyndon B. Johnson pushed the act through Congress.

WE
DEMAND

EQUAL
RIGHTS
NOW!

TALK ABOUT IT

◎ Why do you think civil rights leaders made sure all protests were nonviolent? Do you think this was the right approach? Why or why not?

◎ What do you think was the most important contribution made by young people and students during the 1950s and 1960s civil rights movement?

◎ Civil rights workers wanted Congress to know that a great many people believed in the Civil Rights Bill. What other ways could they have used to show this besides holding a huge protest march?

WRITE ABOUT IT

Many people who took part in the March on Washington are still alive today. Find someone, perhaps a member of your family, who was there. Interview the individual about what happened at the march and how he or she felt about it. Write a brief summary of the March on Washington, using that person's viewpoint.

ECHOES
OF CIVIL RIGHTS

All kinds of people–rich and poor, African American, and others–have taken part in the struggle for African American equality. Those who worked for the passage of the Civil Rights Act of 1964 achieved a great deal. What characteristics did these people have that made their efforts so successful? What can we learn from them? In what other countries are people struggling for equal rights today?

The goal of the civil rights movement during the 1950s and 1960s was to make sure all people in the United States shared equal rights. The African Americans who pushed this movement forward made sacrifices for their cause. They even put their own lives in danger. What do you think America would be like today if these Americans hadn't struggled for equal rights? How might your life be different if the Civil Rights Act had not become the law of the land? ◪

BRIDGING THE YEARS

After 1965, the civil rights movement took new directions. People began to consider the problems of the African Americans in the North as well as the South. New efforts were directed at gaining equal rights in housing, jobs, and the justice system for all minority groups.

Civil rights workers turned their attention more to social problems. They looked for ways to fight the poverty, homelessness, crime, and drug abuse that trouble every American life. However, the struggle to gain "life, liberty, and the pursuit of happiness" as promised in the Constitution still goes on.

A rich heritage of hard work, belief in justice, and caring for their fellow man can be seen in the African American community today. All phases of American life have benefited from African American achievement. This achievement provides the tools for meeting the challenges of the future.

▲*DR. MAE JEMISON*
First African American woman astronaut

▼*MUHAMMAD ALI*—World Heavyweight Champion

▲*SPIKE LEE*
Motion picture producer

▲ *Rev. JESSE JACKSON*—First African American man to run for President

▲*TONI MORRISON*
Won 1988 Pulitzer Prize
for Literature

▲*SHIRLEY CHISHOLM*
First African American woman
in Congress

▼*L. DOUGLAS WILDER*
First elected African American governor

▼*FLORENCE
GRIFFITH-JOYNER*
Olympic gold medalist

▲*GENERAL COLIN L. POWELL*
Former chairman of the Joint Chiefs
of Staff

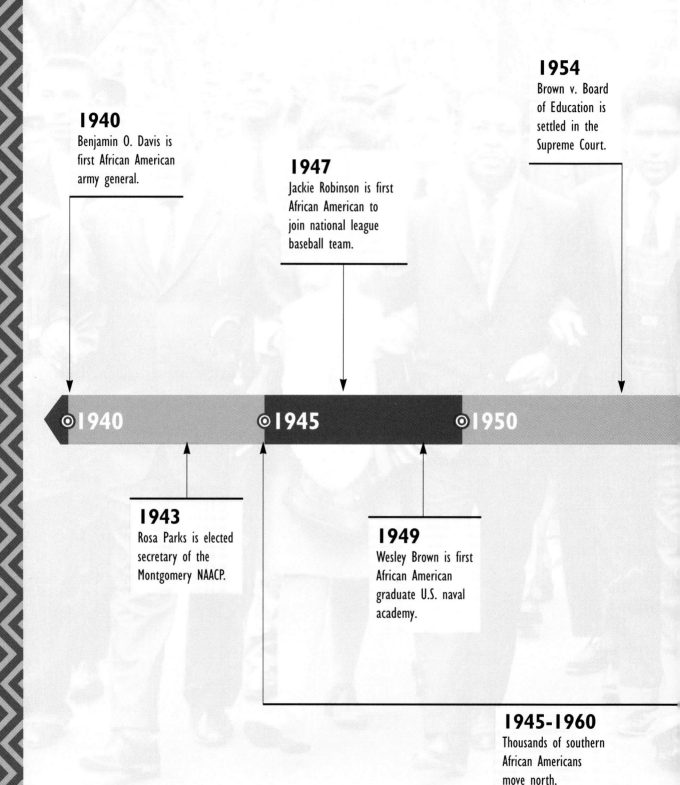

1954
Brown v. Board of Education is settled in the Supreme Court.

1940
Benjamin O. Davis is first African American army general.

1947
Jackie Robinson is first African American to join national league baseball team.

◎1940   ◎1945   ◎1950

1943
Rosa Parks is elected secretary of the Montgomery NAACP.

1949
Wesley Brown is first African American graduate U.S. naval academy.

1945-1960
Thousands of southern African Americans move north.

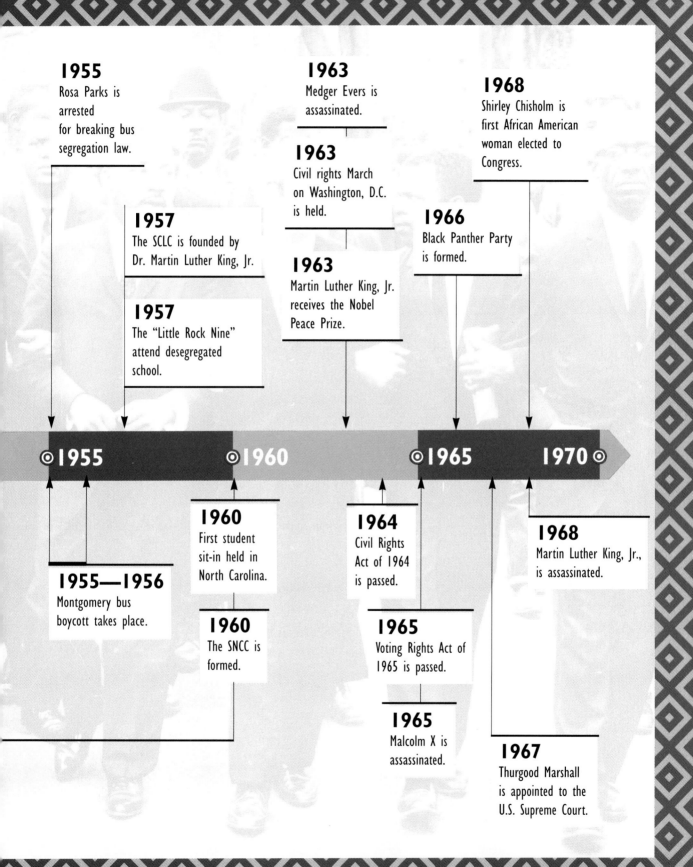

1955
Rosa Parks is arrested for breaking bus segregation law.

1963
Medger Evers is assassinated.

1968
Shirley Chisholm is first African American woman elected to Congress.

1957
The SCLC is founded by Dr. Martin Luther King, Jr.

1963
Civil rights March on Washington, D.C. is held.

1966
Black Panther Party is formed.

1957
The "Little Rock Nine" attend desegregated school.

1963
Martin Luther King, Jr. receives the Nobel Peace Prize.

◎**1955** ◎**1960** ◎**1965** **1970** ◎

1955—1956
Montgomery bus boycott takes place.

1960
First student sit-in held in North Carolina.

1964
Civil Rights Act of 1964 is passed.

1968
Martin Luther King, Jr., is assassinated.

1960
The SNCC is formed.

1965
Voting Rights Act of 1965 is passed.

1965
Malcolm X is assassinated.

1967
Thurgood Marshall is appointed to the U.S. Supreme Court.

GLOSSARY

amendment • *(uh MEHND muhnt)* • A change or an addition to a bill or law.

assassinate • *(uh SASS uh nayt)* • To murder a government official for political reasons.

Black Muslims • *(BLAK MUHZ lumz)* • African Americans who follow the religion of Islam.

boycott • *(BOI kaht)* • To refuse to use or buy something until a demanded action is taken, or a requirement is changed.

Civil Rights Act • *(SIH vul RYETS AKT)* • The equal rights legislation submitted to Congress during the presidency of John F. Kennedy that dealt with outlawing segregation in the United States.

civil rights movement • *(SIH vul RYETS MOOV muhnt)* • A movement of the 1950s and 1960s to win equal rights for African Americans.

colored • *(CUH lurd)* • An old-fashioned term for referring to African Americans.

discrimination • *(dihs skrim uh NAY shun)* • Unjust treatment based on a characteristic or belief people have.

integration • *(in tuh GRAY shun)* • The equal treatment of people of all races.

Jim Crow laws • *(JIM KRO LAHZ)* • Laws that kept African Americans separate and did not provide for their equal rights.

justice • *(JUHS tis)* • A judge who serves on the Supreme Court.

Ku Klux Klan • *(KOO KLUHKS KLAN)* • A secret society formed in the South after the Civil War. The group, made up of whites only, uses violence to support policies of white superiority.

Mecca • *(MEH ka)* • A city in Saudi Arabia that is the holiest city for followers of the religion of Islam.

MIA • Montgomery Improvement Association.

NAACP • National Association for the Advancement of Colored People.

Negro • *(NEE groh)* • Another word for African American; first used by the Spanish.

picket • *(PIH keht)* • To stand or walk outside a business to protest something the business is doing.

SCLC • Southern Christian Leadership Conference.

segregation • *(seh gruh GAY shun)* • The separation of people because of sex, race, belief, or religion.

sharecropper • *(Shayr crah pur)* • A farmer who lives and grows crops on someone else's land for a share of the crops.

sit-in • *(SIHT IHN)* • A form of protest in the civil rights movement in which people sat where they previously had not been allowed.

SNCC • Student Nonviolent Coordinating Committee

Supreme Court • *(suh PREEM CORT)* • The highest court in the United States.

test case • *(TEHST KAYS)* • A legal case brought before the Supreme Court that would ask the court to look at whether or not a particular law was a fair one.

Index